Raising Amelia
A Feathery Tale of Love
for kidlets big and small
written and illustrated by Nancy H. Taylor

Nancy H. Taylor

Amelia's Mum & Illustrator of

"Raising Amelia",

a Feathery Tale of Love

Library and Archives Canada Cataloguing in Publication

Taylor, Nancy H. (Nancy Helena), 1954-
    Raising Amelia : a feathery tale of love for kidlets big
and small / written and illustrated by Nancy H. Taylor.

ISBN 978-0-9918018-0-0

        I. Title.

PS8639.A9535R34 2013   jC813'.6   C2013-901381-4

Book design and layout: Nancy H. Taylor, Cranberry Blewe Design
Printed and bound in Canada by Island Blue / Printorium Bookworks

For Haggsie

For Dick and Virgina Brown
and those who seek to love
wild hearts

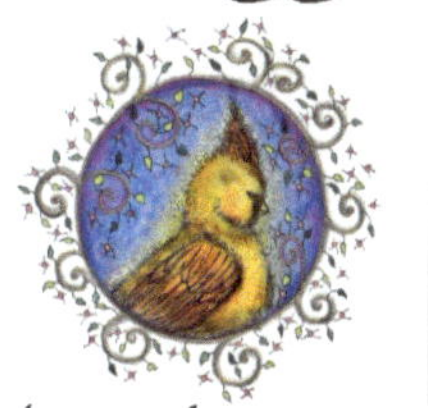

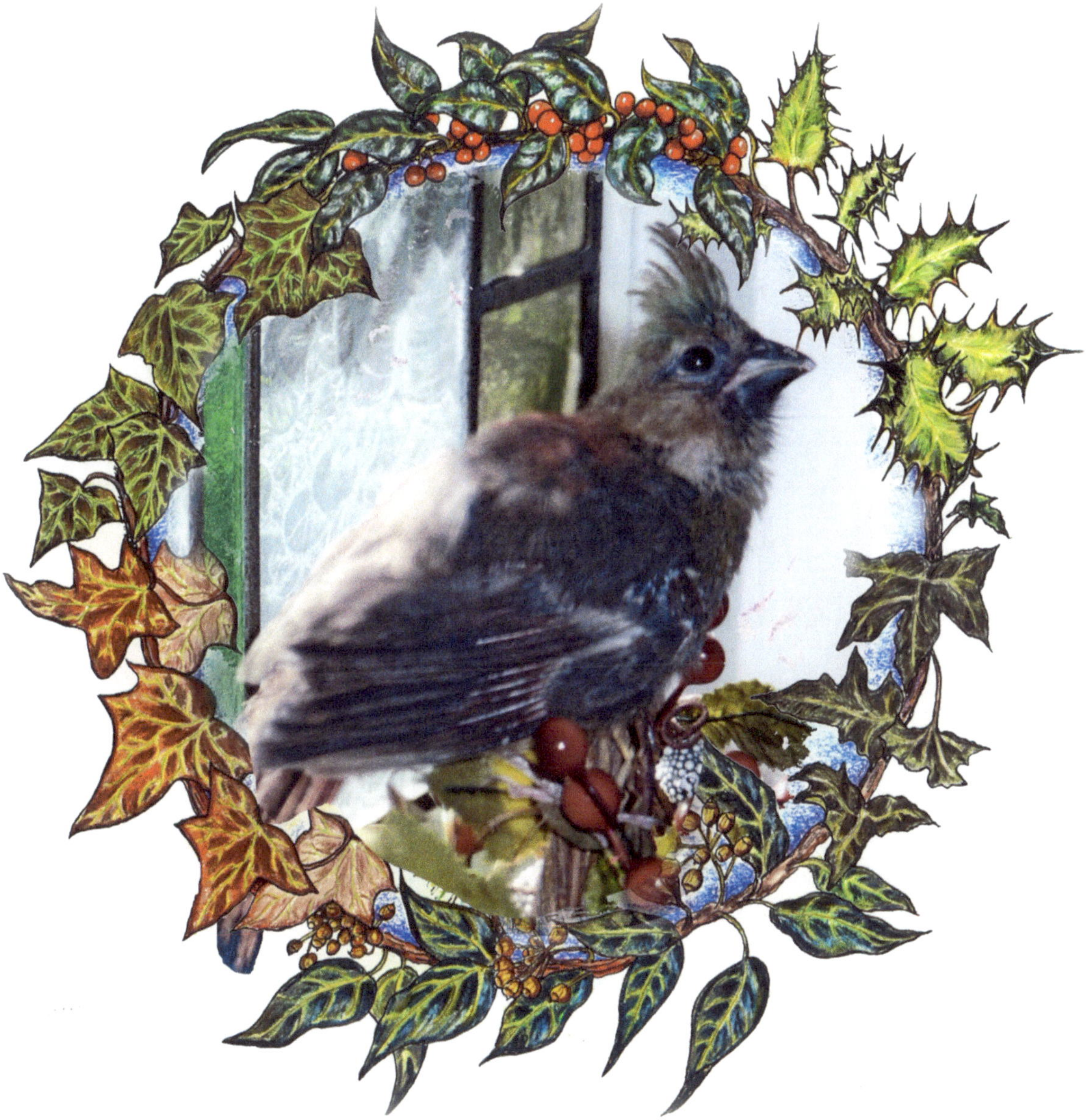

The Real Amelia

Raising Amelia

In the great green cool dark of a cedar hedge a little bird was born. The Spring evening air brought the sweet promise of growing things but there was still a coolness in the breeze. She snuggled into her nest, her body pressed against her brothers and sisters for warmth.

All of a sudden her brothers and sisters began to chirp and tweetle, "Here! Here! HERE! Was there some dinner coming? She tried to stand to see what the noise was all about. She was not very strong and her little legs swayed as she tottered, fighting to keep her balance. "If I could just climb up on the edge, " she thought, "I could see what all the excitement is about." But as she pulled herself up to see, her brothers and sisters jostled her and she lost her balance. She gave a frightened little tweetle, "Help!" and over she went.

The ground was cold and hard and she missed the warm musty twiglet smell of her nest. "Surely mother or father will help me" she thought. As time passed, the sun began to journey over the horizon and the air turned shades of cool blue and lavender. She was cold and no longer had the strength to tweetle for help. Feeling weak and sleepy she closed her eyes and waited.

Now about this time Betsy Boot and her husband
were out for their evening walk. They set off up the
street in the deepening twilight. As they passed a
long, green, cool, dark cedar hedge, Mrs. Boot saw
a baby bird on the grass just on the edge of the
darkened recesses of the hedge. It's body was
cold and its little eyes were shut.
"Oh you poor
wee treasure
you've fallen
from your
nest!" Mr. and
Mrs. Boot
looked and
looked but
they could not
see the cleverly
hidden nest in
the green,
cool, dark
of the cedar
hedge.

Mrs. Boot picked the baby up and felt that her little body was cool. "Oh dear!, I think she's already past help" cried Mrs. Boot. But as she moved to set her back down she thought she saw a little leg move ever so softly; a movement more like a sigh or a soft whisper.

"She's still alive!" That night Amelia slept in a little basket lined with a soft sock on the plate warmer of the stove. Betsy had made her a supper of egg yolk with warm water and a little honey and fed her ever so gently with an eye dropper.

The next morning the house was filled with Amelia's
tweetles for food. And so for the next few weeks Mrs.
Boot fed her and fed her and fed her. Every hour
Amelia was hungry and wanted to eat. Mrs. Boot had
a new found respect for bird parents as she now knew
it was no easy job to raise a little one. Amelia began
to change in a wondrous way. From the downy tufts
on her back little feathers began to sprout. From her
fuzzy bottom shaped like the end of your big toe, her
long graceful tail feathers fanned out.

The most amazing change of all was on top of her head. Here, a beautiful crest of feathers appeared which, when standing up, made Amelia look very regal indeed!

In no time at all, Amelia outgrew her little basket
and when she was strong enough, Mrs. Boot let her
perch on her finger and took her around the
house. Amelia noticed that her wings were almost
full grown. She fluttered them to show off and realized with a tweetle of joy that she felt as light as
air! How Wonderful!! Soon she was ready for her
first flight. She found a spot in the living room
where she wanted to fly, measured once, twice and
off she went. Amelia's tiny breast shuddered with
excitement and her crest glowed with pride.

Betsy soon realized that Amelia
needed a safe place to stay or she
might get hurt. Amelia's new home
was large and lovely with fresh
leafy perches, two baskets for
seeds and a little door. It was
even shaped like a house!

Each morning Betsy brought
Amelia garlands of fresh flowers
and live twigs to perch on. Amelia
no longer thought of the
outdoors. She had love and food
and toys to enjoy each and every
day. This would have suited her
forever but there was one
problem. Her tail feathers grew
longer and longer until they were
as long as Amelia herself. Her
grownup feathers were replacing
all her baby feathers.
She was growing up.

One fine summer day, Betsy went out to visit a friend and left Amelia in her little house in the Garden hanging safe and high out of harms way to enjoy the silky summer breezes and hear the sounds of the wild birds as they went about their busy day. Amelia was often taken outside with Mrs. Boot when she did her gardening and it was one of her favourite things. Betsy arrived home knowing that Amelia would be hungry.

Her eyes stared wide in disbelief - Amelia's house was empty! Somehow the little door had come open. In a panic Mrs. Boot called for Amelia. At first there was no reply and Betsy's eyes filled with tears. "She's lost and she can't fly very well or feed herself. Oh Amelia, where are you?" Then, through all the other noise of the street Mrs. Boot recognized Amelia's panicked tweetles for help. She followed the sounds to find her precious Amelia in a neighbour's yard in some bushes. There was a tall fence around the yard and Betsy couldn't get to her.

She popped her head over the fence and called to Amelia. To her joy Amelia flew over and sat on the fence top. Very gently, Betsy picked her up and gave her a little kiss on her head and placed her in her house. At that moment Mrs. Boot realized just how much she loved Amelia - she had almost lost her and she never wanted that to happen again.

The summer days passed into weeks and Amelia now ate birdseed and berries and had grown into a fine sleek shape. Her flying was becoming very accomplished and she was free most of the day to fly about the house. As Amelia got bigger the house became smaller and smaller. Betsy began to recognize something different about Amelia. Her old toys didn't make her happy anymore. "Why was she not happy anymore?" she wondered.

She has food and toys and a lovely warm house but something is missing. Mrs. Boot knew what it meant. Amelia was a wild bird and she had to have a chance to live her life wild and free. As much as it broke Betsy's heart to think about it she knew she had to prepare to let Amelia go.

And so, one day Betsy took Amelia in the car. Amelia heard Mrs. Boot's voice and it sounded different. It sounded very sad. There was a time she was alone in her home with a cloth over it so she couldn't see what was going on. When the cloth was taken off and her door opened she was in a very large house with live branches and perches and - other birds! Up to that time Amelia had not known she was a bird. Now, she needed to be accepted by the other birds or she would never be able to be free.

For days Amelia called and called for Mrs. Boot but Betsy never came. Gradually, she made friends with the other birds and she thought less and less of Mrs. Boot. She was becoming a wild bird and her adventures in the wild would soon begin.In the meantime, Betsy puttered about the house with a heavy heart. Just the call of a cardinal would make her eyes fill with tears as she missed her tiny friend. Mrs. Boot had taken Amelia to a wildlife shelter to help her and the other birds return to the wild after recovering from injuries. Betsy called every week to make sure Amelia was doing well.

At last the day came when the shelter called to
say that Amelia had been released into the wild
on a farm out in the country with her other bird
friends. This time Betsy cried tears of joy for
all she had worked for had come to pass.

Now, the story could finish here, but there is one more tale to tell. The following Spring - almost a year to the day she found Amelia, Mr. and Mrs. Boot were having their early morning tea in front of the fire. It was just coming dawn and they heard outside their window the beautiful clear song of a cardinal. Betsy walked softly to the window and looked out to see where the bird was perched.

On the top of a little evergreen tree in the yard sat the the carolling bird. Betsy knew at that moment it was Amelia.

She had returned to give Betsy the most
precious gift she could. She sang with all her
heart for the one who had loved her enough
to set her free.